THE AMERICAN GIRLS

17 *74*

FELICITY, a spunky, spritely colonial girl,
full of energy and independence

18 *24*

JOSEFINA, an Hispanic girl whose heart and
hopes are as big as the New Mexico sky

18  *54*

KIRSTEN, a pioneer girl of strength and
spirit who settles on the frontier

18 *64*

ADDY, a courageous girl determined to be
free in the midst of the Civil War

19  *04*

SAMANTHA, a bright Victorian beauty, an
orphan raised by her wealthy grandmother

19  *34*

KIT, a clever, resourceful girl facing the
Great Depression with spirit and determination

19  *44*

MOLLY, who schemes and dreams on the
home front during World War Two

1934
KIT
LEARNS
A LESSON
A School Story

BY VALERIE TRIPP
ILLUSTRATIONS WALTER RANE
VIGNETTES SUSAN MCALILEY

American Girl™

Printed in the United States of America.
00 01 02 03 04 05 06 07 08 QWT 12 11 10 9 8 7 6 5 4 3 2 1

The American Girls Collection®, Kit™, Kit Kittredge™, and American Girl®
are trademarks of Pleasant Company.

PICTURE CREDITS
The following individuals and organizations have generously given
permission to reprint images contained in "Looking Back":
pp. 62-63—Courtesy of the Wood family (classroom photo); courtesy of Frances Pederson
Hall (report cards and merit pins); *Palmer Method Handwriting*, McGraw-Hill Companies;
cover, *Ohio Valley Pioneers* by Harry Edmund Danford; cover, *Stories in Trees* published by
Lyons & Carnahan; cover, *Tales & Travels*, Simon & Schuster; pp. 64-65—Records of Soil
Conservation Service/National Archives, NA 114-SD-5089 (farm); Library of Congress (family
in car and girl with cotton sack); *Chicago Daily News*/Illinois State Historical Society (protesting
teachers); © Bettmann/CORBIS (single woman protester); pp. 66-67—*The Cincinnati Post* (teacher
and headline); from the book *Public Schools in Hard Times*, published by Harvard University
Press, photo by Marion Post Wolcott (crowded classroom); Brown Brothers (breadline);
courtesy of Frances Pederson Hall (rhythm band).

Edited by Tamara England and Judith Woodburn
Designed by Myland McRevey, Justin Packard, Ingrid Slamer, and Jane S. Varda
Art Directed by Laura Moberly and Ingrid Slamer
Cover Background by Mike Wimmer

Library of Congress Cataloging-in-Publication Data

Tripp, Valerie, 1951-
Kit learns a lesson : a school story / by Valerie Tripp ;
illustrations Walter Rane ; vignettes Susan McAliley.

p. cm. — (The American girls collection)

Summary: In 1932 Kit finds that she has hard lessons to learn about the Depression, both at
home, where she is helping her mother run a boarding house while her father looks for a
new job, and at school, where a fight spoils the preparations for the Thanksgiving pageant.
ISBN 1-58485-121-X (hc.). — ISBN 1-58485-018-3 (pbk.)
1. Depressions—1929—Juvenile fiction.
[1. Depressions—1929—Fiction. 2. Schools—Fiction.
3. Thanksgiving Day—Fiction. 4. Boardinghouses—Fiction.]
I. Rane, Walter, ill. II. Title. III. Series.
PZ7.T7363 Kg 2000 [Fic]—dc21 99-086466

FOR JILL DAVIDSON MARTINEZ,
WITH LOVE

TABLE OF CONTENTS

DAD
*Kit's father, a
businessman facing
the problems of the
Great Depression.*

MOTHER
*Kit's mother, who takes
care of her family and
their home with strength
and determination.*

KIT
*A clever, resourceful
girl who helps her family
cope with the dark days
of the Depression.*

CHARLIE
*Kit's affectionate and
supportive sixteen-
year-old brother.*

**UNCLE
HENDRICK**
*Mother's wealthy and
disapproving uncle.*

MRS. HOWARD
Mother's garden club friend, who is a guest in the Kittredge home.

STIRLING HOWARD
Mrs. Howard's son, whose delicate health hides surprising strengths.

RUTHIE SMITHENS
Kit's best friend, who is loyal, understanding, and generous.

ROGER
A know-it-all boy in Kit's class.

MESSAGES

"Hey, Kit, wake up."

Kit Kittredge opened one eye and saw
her brother Charlie at the foot of her
bed. She put her pillow over her head and groaned,
"Go *away*."

"Can't do that," said Charlie cheerfully. "Not till
I'm sure you're up and at 'em." He turned on the
lamp. "Come on, Squirt. Time to get to work."

Kit groaned again, but she sat up. "I'm awake,"
she yawned.

"Good," said Charlie. He tilted his head. "What's
that funny sound?"

Kit listened. *Plink. Plinkplinkplink!* "Oh," she
said. "The roof leaks."

"Why don't you ask Dad to fix it?" asked Charlie. "I'm sure he could."

"Well, it only leaks when it rains," said Kit.

"No kidding," said Charlie.

"Besides, I like the plinking sound," Kit said. "It's like someone's sending me a message in a secret code that uses plinks instead of dots and dashes." In the adventure stories Kit loved to read, people often sent messages in secret codes, and Kit was a girl who was always on the lookout for excitement.

"*Plinkplinkplink*," said Charlie. "That means 'Get up, Kit.'"

"Okay, okay!" laughed Kit as she got out of bed. "I get the message!"

"At last," said Charlie. "See you later." He waved and disappeared down the stairs. Charlie had to leave very early every day to get to his job loading newspapers onto trucks, but he always woke Kit and said good-bye before he left.

It was cold in the attic this rainy November morning. Kit shivered and dressed quickly. Mornings got off to a fast start at the Kittredge house these days. Because of the Depression, Kit's dad had lost his job back in August. To bring in money, Kit's family had turned their home into a boarding house. The boarders paid money to rent rooms and have meals there. Mother was *very* particular about having their breakfast ready on time.

As Kit hurriedly tied her shoes, she saw that someone had moved her typewriter from one side of her desk to the other. *I bet Dad used my typewriter,* she thought. *He probably wrote a letter to ask about a job.* Kit sighed. Before Dad lost his job and they started taking in boarders, Kit used to love to type newspapers that told Dad what had happened at home while he was away at work. She promised herself that the day he got a new job, she'd make a newspaper with a huge headline that said, 'Hurray for Dad! Bye-Bye, Boarders!' Kit could not *wait* for that day. She did not like having the boarders in the house *at all*.

The thought of that headline cheered Kit as she went downstairs to the second floor to face her morning chores. Her first stop was the bathroom, where she fished three of Dad's socks out of the laundry basket. Teetering first on one foot, then on the other, Kit put a sock over each shoe. She put the third sock over her right hand like a mitten. Then Kit propped the laundry basket against her hip and peeked out the door to be sure the coast was clear. It was. Kit took a running start, then *swoosh!* She skated down the hallway, dusting the floor with her sock-covered feet and giving the table in the hall a quick swipe with her sock-covered hand.

Kit skated fast. She could already hear the boarders rising and making the annoying noises they made every morning. As she skated past Mr. Peck's room, she heard him blowing his nose: *Honkhonk h-o-n-k! Honkhonk h-o-n-k!* It sounded to Kit like a goose honking the tune of "Jingle Bells." The two lady boarders were chirping to each other in twittery bursts of words and laughter. Next door to them, in what used to be Kit's room, Mrs. Howard was bleating and baaing over her son Stirling like a mother sheep over her lamb. *A chirp, chirp here and a baa, baa there! It's like living on Old MacDonald's Farm, for Pete's sake!* Kit thought crossly. She skated to the top of the stairs, sat, peeled off the socks, and put them back in the laundry basket. Then she climbed onto the banister and polished it by sliding down it sideways.

She landed with a thud at the foot of the stairs and found a surprise waiting for her: Mother.

"Oh! Good morning, Mother!" said Kit.

Mother crossed her arms over her chest. "Is that how you do your chores every day?" she asked. "Skating and sliding?"

"Uh . . . well, yes," said Kit.

"No wonder the hallway is always so dusty. Not to mention Dad's socks," said Mother. She sighed a sigh that sounded weary for so early in the morning. "Dear, I thought you understood that we've all got to work hard to make our boarding house a success.

Your chores are not a game. Is that clear?"

"Yes, Mother," said Kit.

"I'd appreciate it if you would dust more carefully from now on," said Mother. She managed a small smile. "And so would Dad's socks."

Kit felt sheepish. "Should I dust the hall again now?" she asked.

"I'm afraid there's no time," said Mother. "I'll try to get to it myself later. Right now I need your help with breakfast. The boarders will be down any minute. Come along."

"Okay," Kit said as she followed Mother into the kitchen. To herself she groused, *The boarders! It's all their fault. Mother never scolded me about things like dusting before they came, because I never had boring chores to do!* Kit knew her skate-and-slide method of dusting was slapdash, but she'd thought that nobody had noticed the dust left in the corners—except maybe persnickety Mrs. Howard. She should've known Mother would see it, too.

Mother wanted everything to be as nice as possible for the boarders. She insisted that the table be set beautifully for every meal. She went to great pains to make the food look nice, too, though there wasn't much of it. Dad went downtown nearly every day and brought home a loaf of bread and sometimes cans of fruits and vegetables. But even so, Mother had to invent ways to stretch the food so that there was enough. This morning Kit watched Mother cut the toasted bread into pretty triangles. Then, after Kit spooned oatmeal into a bowl, Mother put a thin slice of canned peach on top.

"That looks nice," said Kit. "The toast does, too."

"Just some tricks I've learned," Mother said. "Cutting the toast in triangles makes it look like there's more than there really is. And I'm hoping the peach slices will distract our guests from the fact that we've had oatmeal four times this week already. But it's cheap and it's filling."

"Humph!" said Kit as she plopped oatmeal into another bowl. "Oatmeal's good enough for *them*."

"Hush, Kit!" said Mother. She glanced at the door to the dining room as if the boarders might have heard. "You mustn't say that. We've got to keep our boarders happy. We need them to stay. In fact, we need more."

"*More* boarders?" asked Kit, horrified. "Oh, Mother, why?"

"Because," said Mother, sounding weary again, "even with Charlie's earnings and the rent from the boarders, we don't have enough money to cover our expenses. We need at least two more boarders to make ends meet."

"But where would we put them?" asked Kit. "No one would pay to share my attic. The roof leaks! And Charlie's sleeping porch is going to be freezing cold this winter."

"Yes," agreed Mother. "The sleeping porch should be enclosed, but we don't have any money for lumber."

sleeping porch

"Anyway," said Kit, "it'd be silly to go changing the house all around and filling it with boarders when I bet Dad is going to get another job any day now. Didn't he say he's going downtown again today to have lunch with a business friend?"

"Mmmhmm," said Mother, taking the oatmeal spoon from Kit.

"Probably it's an interview!" said Kit. She crossed her fingers on both hands. "Oh, I hope Dad gets a job!" she wished aloud.

"That," said Mother, "would be a dream

come true." She handed the heavy breakfast tray
to Kit, took off her apron, and smoothed her hair.
"Meanwhile, all we have going for us is this house
and our own hard work. We must do everything we
can to make sure our boarders stay. We can't let them
see us worried and moping. So! Shoulders back, chin
up, and put on a cheery morning face, please."

Kit forced her lips into a stiff smile.

"I guess that will have to do," said Mother
briskly. She put on a smile too, pushed open the
door, and walked into the dining room like an actress
making an entrance on a stage. Dad and all the
boarders were seated at the table. "Good morning,
everyone!" Mother said.

"Good morning!" they all answered.

Kit's smile turned into a real one when she saw
Dad, who was wearing his best suit and looking
very handsome. He winked at her as if to send her
a message that said, *It really **is** a good morning now
that I've seen you.*

Miss Hart and Miss Finney, the two lady
boarders, cooed with pleasure when Kit set their
peachy oatmeal before them. Kit was careful not
to spill. Miss Hart and Miss Finney were nurses.

"Good morning, everyone!" Mother said.

Their starched uniforms were as white as blank pieces of paper before a story was written on them. *I bet Miss Hart and Miss Finney have plenty of interesting stories to tell about their patients at the hospital*, thought Kit. *Maybe they've had daring nursing adventures, like Florence Nightingale and Clara Barton. What great newspaper headlines those adventures would make!*

Then Kit scolded herself for being curious. Miss Hart and Miss Finney must remain blank pages! Kit did not want to like them. She did not want to be interested in them or in Mr. Peck, either, even though he played a double bass as big as a bear and had a beard and was so tall he reminded Kit of Little John in her favorite book, *Robin Hood.* They would probably all turn out to be dull anyway, just as disappointing as tidy Mrs. Howard and skinny Stirling. They were *not* friends. They were only boarders, and they wouldn't be around for very long. As soon as Dad got a new job, they'd leave. Kit thought back to the wish she'd made and rewrote it in her head. *I should have added the word* **soon**, she thought. *I hope Dad gets a job* **soon.**

As Kit sat down at her place, she saw Dad slip his toast onto Stirling's plate. Stirling's mother saw, too, and started to fuss. "Oh, Mr. Kittredge!" said Mrs. Howard to Dad. "You're too generous! And Stirling's digestion is so delicate! He can't eat so much breakfast. It's a shame to waste it."

"Don't worry, Mrs. Howard," joked Dad. "Stirling's just helping me be a member of the Clean Plate Club. I'm having lunch with a friend today. I don't want to ruin my appetite."

Stirling, who was Kit's age but so short he looked much younger, didn't say a word. But Kit noticed that he wolfed down his own toast and Dad's, too, pretty fast. *Delicate digestion, my eye,* thought Kit.

"Goodness, Mr. Kittredge," Miss Finney piped up. "Last night at dinner you said you weren't hungry because you'd had a big lunch. Those lunches must be feasts!"

"They are indeed," said Dad.

Just then, Mother brought in the morning mail. She handed a couple of letters to Dad and one fat envelope to Miss Finney, who got a letter from her boyfriend in Boston practically every day. Kit was trying to imagine what Miss Finney's boyfriend had to say to her in those long letters when Mother said,

"Why, Stirling, dear, look! This letter is for you."

Everyone was quiet as Mother handed Stirling the letter. Even his mother was speechless for once. The tips of Stirling's ears turned as pink as boiled shrimp. He looked at the envelope with his name and address typed on it, then eagerly ripped the envelope open, tearing it apart in his haste to get the letter out and read it.

Mrs. Howard recovered. "Who's it from, lamby?" she asked.

Stirling smiled a watery, timid-looking smile. "It's from Father," he answered. His odd husky voice sounded unsure, as if he himself could hardly believe what he was saying.

"My land!" exclaimed Mrs. Howard, pressing one hand against her heart. "A letter at last! What does he say?"

Stirling read the typewritten letter aloud. "'Dear Son, I haven't got a permanent address yet. I'll write to you when I do, and I'll send more money as soon as I can. Give my love to Mother. Love, Father.'" Stirling handed two ten-dollar bills to his mother. "He sent us this."

13

"Wow!" exclaimed Kit. "Twenty dollars? That's a lot of money!"

Miss Finney and Miss Hart murmured their agreement, and Mr. Peck put down his coffee cup in amazement.

Mrs. Howard was overcome with happiness. In a weak voice she said to Mother, "Margaret, take this," she said as she tried to give Mother one of the ten-dollar bills. "You've been so kind to us. You must share in our lucky day."

"Oh, but—" Mother began.

"I insist," said Mrs. Howard.

Mother hesitated. Then she said, "Thank you." She put the ten-dollar bill in her pocket.

After that, everyone started talking at once about Stirling's startling letter. Everyone but Stirling, that is. Kit saw Stirling read his father's message once more, and then fold the letter very small and hold it in his closed hand.

After breakfast, Dad sat at the kitchen table reading the want ads in the newspaper while Kit and Mother washed the dishes. "Mr. Howard must be doing all right if he can send his wife twenty dollars," Dad said from behind the newspaper. "Maybe Chicago is the place to go. Maybe there are jobs there."

"Chicago *is* a bigger city than Cincinnati," said Mother.

"We'd move to Chicago?" asked Kit. She didn't like the idea of leaving her home and her friends.

"No," said Dad, putting the paper down. "Only I would go."

Kit spun around from the sink so quickly her wet hand left a trail of soapsuds on the kitchen floor. "You'd go without us?" she asked, shocked. "You'd leave us? Oh, Dad, you can't!"

"Now Kit, calm down," said Dad. "It's just an idea. I haven't said I'll go. But if nothing turns up here by Thanksgiving . . ."

"Thanksgiving?" interrupted Kit. "That's only two weeks away!"

"You know how hard your father's been looking for a job here in Cincinnati," said Mother. "Ever since August."

"And he'll find one," said Kit. She looked at her father. "Won't you, Dad? One of those business friends you have lunch with is sure to offer you a job any day now, right?"

"Kit, sweetheart," Dad started to answer, then stopped. He picked up the paper and went back to his reading. "Right," he said. "Any day now."

As Kit turned back to the dishes, she thought, *When I wished for Dad to get a job soon, I didn't mean in Chicago!* In her head, she rewrote the message of her wish again. Now it was: *I hope Dad gets a job **soon**, and **here in Cincinnati.***

PILGRIMS AND INDIANS

As they walked to school that morning, Kit told her best friend Ruthie about changing her wish for Dad. The girls huddled under Ruthie's umbrella. They ignored Stirling, who trailed along behind them like a puny, pitiful puppy. "I didn't realize a wish had to be so specific," said Kit.

"Oh, yes," said Ruthie. "You have to be *very* careful what you say in a wish. Otherwise it'll come true, but not the way you meant it to. That happens a lot in fairy tales." Ruthie had read hundreds of fairy tales because she was interested in princesses. "Also, you usually have to work hard to *deserve* a wish to come true. You have to do something brave or impossible, or make a giant, noble sacrifice. And you have to wait. Wishes take time. Years, in some cases."

"Thanksgiving's only two weeks from now," said Kit. "I'm afraid that if Dad doesn't get a job here by then, he'll go away to Chicago."

"Chicago," repeated Ruthie. "He might as well go to the moon."

"I don't want *Dad* to leave," said Kit. "I want the *boarders* to leave."

Ruthie tugged on one of the straps of Kit's book bag and tilted her head toward Stirling. Kit realized that once again she'd spoken without thinking. She was pretty sure that Stirling already knew she wanted him and the other boarders to leave. Still, it wasn't nice to say so in front of him. Kit wouldn't have if she'd remembered that he was there. He was just so *invisible*.

All morning at school Kit tried not to think about how awful it would be to watch the boarders sitting around the table gobbling Thanksgiving turkey if she knew that Dad was going to leave. She could hardly bear listening to Roger, a show-offy boy in her class, answer a question about the first Thanksgiving that their teacher, Mr. Fisher, had asked.

"The first Thanksgiving was in 1621," said Roger. "The Pilgrims invited the Indians to a feast to celebrate their successful harvest. We have turkey at Thanksgiving because the Pilgrims served the Indians four wild turkeys, and we call it Thanksgiving because the Indians were thankful to the Pilgrims for being generous and sharing their food."

Kit couldn't stand it. She shot her hand up into the air and waved it.

"Yes, Kit?" said Mr. Fisher.

"Roger's got the story backwards," said Kit. "It's called Thanksgiving because the Pilgrims gave the feast to thank the Indians."

Roger snorted.

Kit wasn't the least bit intimidated by Roger. "The Pilgrims would've starved to death if it weren't for the Indians," she said. "The Indians taught the Pilgrims to plant corn and gave them supplies and help. I think that was pretty nice of the Indians, considering that the Pilgrims had barged into their land where they'd been living happily by themselves for a long time." As Kit spoke, she realized that this year, more than ever before, she had tremendous

Kit shot her hand up into the air and waved it.

sympathy for the Indians. She knew how it felt to have a bunch of strangers living with you and eating your food and expecting your help when you didn't want them there in the first place!

"Well!" said Mr. Fisher. "Thank you, Kit."

It made Kit feel a little better to have pleased Mr. Fisher. She liked him, but they had gotten off on the wrong foot the first day of school when Mr. Fisher called on Kit to read aloud in reading group. Kit hadn't known what page they were on because she'd read ahead and was busy thinking up better endings to the stories.

Mr. Fisher was cross with her then, but he was happy with her now. "Kit makes a good point," he said. "The Indians took pity on the Pilgrims and shared what little they had. It's important to help both friends and strangers when times are hard. We see this all around us today, because of the Depression. Who can give me examples of ways that our families and friends and neighbors are helping one another, and strangers, too?"

"When hoboes come to our back door," said Ruthie, "my mother always gives them sandwiches and coffee."

"At our church there's a box of old shoes for people to take if they need them," said a boy named Tom.

"My cousin sent me a winter coat she'd out-grown," said a girl named Mabel.

Kit was surprised to see Stirling raise his hand. He'd almost never done so before. Stirling was new to the class and the school because he had moved into Kit's house only last summer. He didn't know anyone but Kit and Ruthie, and he was so quiet he was easy to forget.

"Sometimes people get kicked out of their house because they can't pay the rent," Stirling said in his deep voice that always surprised Kit, coming as it did from such a pip-squeak. "And friends are nice and invite them to live in their house with them."

"Oh, so that's why you live with Kit," brayed Roger. "I thought you two were married!"

The class snickered as Roger made kissing noises. Stirling slouched in his seat. Kit shook her fist at Roger, but she was mad at Stirling, too. *Stirling should have kept his mouth shut!* she thought.

"That will do, Roger," said Mr. Fisher. "I'll wait

for quiet, boys and girls." He waited until the snickering stopped, then asked, "Who can give me more examples of how we're helping one another?"

"Soup kitchens serve free meals to people who can't buy food," said a girl named Dorothy. "And some soup kitchens also give people groceries to take home to their families."

"Yes," said Mr. Fisher. "Now, as you all know, Thanksgiving is coming soon. I'd like our class to do its part to help the hungry. So if you can, please bring in an item of food. It doesn't have to be anything big. An apple or a potato will do. I know most of us don't have much food to spare. But if we all chip in, we can make a Thanksgiving basket and donate it to a soup kitchen."

The students murmured among themselves, but without much enthusiasm. They'd all seen soup kitchens with long lines of people waiting outside them. Kit had once seen a man in a soup line faint on the street from hunger. She knew that soup kitchens were for people who had been without work for so long that they had no money or hope or pride left, and who were so desperate that they had to accept free food.

"My father says that people who go to soup kitchens should be ashamed," said Roger, full of bluster. "They're bums."

"They're not bums," said Ruthie. "Most of them are perfectly nice, normal people who happen to be down on their luck. I think we should feel sorry for them."

"My father says they're just too lazy to work," said Roger. "And now that Franklin Roosevelt's been elected, people will expect the government to take care of them. My father says it'll ruin our country."

Franklin Roosevelt

Kit grew hot under the collar listening to Roger and thinking of how hard Dad was trying to find a job. "People aren't too lazy to work," she said. "They'd work if they could find a job. But jobs are hard to find."

Mr. Fisher nodded. "Right here in Cincinnati," he said, "one out of three workers is unemployed, which means they don't have a job. One out of three. What fraction is that?"

"One-third," said Tom.

"That's correct," said Mr. Fisher.

24

One out of three? thought Kit. Unemployment was a lot worse than she'd thought! Just for a shivery second, her absolute confidence that Dad would find a job in Cincinnati was shaken a little bit. Maybe he really would have to go to Chicago! Then Kit spoke to herself firmly. *No!* she thought. *Dad is different. He **will** find a job. Any day now. He said so.*

"These are hard times," said Mr. Fisher. "That's why it's especially important to remember the example of the Indians and the Pilgrims. We all have friends or relatives who're struggling to make ends meet. This year many of us will have to do without some of the things we've had in years past."

"But Mr. Fisher," Mabel asked, "we're still going to have a Thanksgiving pageant this year, aren't we?"

"Yes, of course," said Mr. Fisher.

Now the class buzzed with excitement. Everyone loved the pageant!

Mr. Fisher crossed his arms. "I need your attention, boys and girls," he said. The children shushed one another, and Mr. Fisher continued. "The sixth-graders will be the Pilgrims," he said. "The fifth-graders will be the Indians. Our fourth grade is responsible for the scenery." Mr. Fisher

held up a drawing. "Here's a drawing of the
backdrop we'll paint."

The drawing showed four giant turkeys
and a huge cornucopia with fruits and vegetables
spilling out. The turkeys' feathers were all different
colors, and they were not just painted on. They
were made out of bits of paper cut to look like real
feathers, and they were glued onto the turkeys.

"That's good!" said Tom.

"Yes, it is, isn't it?" said Mr. Fisher.

"Who drew it?" asked Dorothy.

"Stirling," said Mr. Fisher.

Everyone twisted around to stare at Stirling.
For the second time that day, Stirling slouched
down in his seat. But this time, no one was
snickering. Everyone, including Kit, was gaping
at Stirling in astonishment.

At lunch Ruthie said, "Stirling is really good at drawing, isn't he, Kit?"

Kit shrugged. "I guess so," she said. She was still annoyed with Stirling for speaking in class and embarrassing her in front of everybody.

"Shh!" said Dorothy. "Here he comes now!"

Stirling was walking toward Kit, his knickers ballooning out over his spindly legs. Kit and Stirling had to share a lunchbox, and every day Stirling came over to the girls' side of the lunchroom to get his sandwich from Kit. Usually, the girls at the table completely ignored Stirling. But today when he came over, several girls squeaked, "Hi, Stirling."

Stirling blushed pinker than ever. "Hi," he mumbled. He took his sandwich and scuttled back to the boys' side. Unfortunately, Roger had spotted Stirling with Kit. He began to whistle "Here Comes the Bride." Kit glowered at Roger, who batted his eyelashes at her across the lunchroom.

"Hey, Kit," said Ruthie, trying to distract her. "Good news! There's some wood left over from our new garage. My father said that you and I can use it for our tree house."

"That's great!" said Kit. She had been sketching tree houses and hoping to build one ever since she'd read *Robin Hood*. She loved the tree houses that Robin and his men built high in the branches of the trees in Sherwood Forest. Kit knew her family had absolutely no money to spend on something as unnecessary as wood for a tree house. So it was lucky that Ruthie's father, who still had a job, was giving away the leftover wood.

"I was thinking," said Ruthie, "you know how your tree house sketches haven't ever really turned out very well?"

"Yes," Kit admitted honestly.

"Well, why don't we ask Stirling to draw a plan for us?" asked Ruthie.

"No!" Kit said. "Gosh, Ruthie! If we let him plan a tree house for us, then when it's built he'll want to come in it and we'll have to let him. He's already invaded my real house. I don't want him in our tree house, too!"

"Okay, okay," said Ruthie. "Don't get all worked up. The tree house doesn't even *exist* yet!"

"I'll ask Dad to help us," said Kit. "He loves building things."

"Sure!" said Ruthie. She grinned. "And he'll be so busy building our tree house, he'll forget all about going away!"

Kit grinned back. "Right!" she said. "How soon can we get that wood?"

SPILLING THE BEANS

A few days later, Kit's class was on the stage in the school auditorium working on the backdrop for the Thanksgiving pageant. Stirling had drawn the outline on big sheets of paper that were pinned to the curtains at the back of the stage. The boys in the class were painting in the fruits and vegetables and the cornucopia. The girls were cutting out paper turkey feathers. Stirling was standing on a stool, gluing the finished feathers onto the outlines of the giant turkeys.

Mr. Fisher was far away, up in the balcony wrestling with the spotlights, and Roger was taking advantage of his absence by being a general pain. He came over and jabbed Stirling with his paintbrush.

"So, Stirling," he said, "when's the wedding for you and Kit?"

It was as if Stirling hadn't heard Roger. He stepped down off his stool and calmly began brushing glue onto another batch of turkey feathers.

Roger turned his back on Stirling. "Hey, Kit," he said. "What's the matter with your boyfriend? He's awful quiet."

"Stirling is *not* my boyfriend," snapped Kit. "He and his mother *pay* to live at our house. They're *boarders*."

"Oh yeah!" Roger drawled. "That's right." He plopped himself down on the stool that Stirling had been using. Loudly and slowly, so that everyone could hear him, Roger said, "I heard that your family is so hard up you're running a boarding house now." He smirked. "And *you're* the maid."

"I am not!" Kit denied hotly. Of course, she *had* been feeling like a maid lately. But she'd never give Roger satisfaction by admitting it.

"That's not what I heard," Roger taunted. "Here's you." He pretended that his paintbrush was a maid's feather duster and he used it to brush some imaginary dust off his arms. Then

31

he stood up, turned, and started to swagger away.

It was then that Kit saw the giant turkey feathers stuck to the seat of Roger's pants! Kit touched Ruthie's arm and pointed at Roger.

Ruthie chortled when she saw the feathers. "Hey, look, everybody!" she called out happily, pointing to Roger's bottom. "Look at Roger—Mr. Turkeypants!"

Everyone looked. The girls screamed with laughter and the boys whistled and clapped. "Hey, Turkeypants!" Ruthie hooted. "Gobble, gobble!" Kit realized with surprise that Stirling must have sneaked the gluey feathers onto the stool just as Roger sat down so they'd stick to his pants when he stood up.

Roger also realized that Stirling was the one who'd tricked him. "You think you're pretty smart, don't you, Stirling?" he said furiously as he pulled off the gluey feathers. "Sticking your stupid turkey feathers on me. Well, at least *my* father hasn't flown the coop and disappeared like yours has!"

By now the whole class was gathered around Kit, Ruthie, Stirling, and Roger. They all looked at Stirling, waiting to hear what he'd say to Roger.

But Stirling didn't say anything, and his silence exasperated Kit. "For your information, birdbrain," she said to Roger, "Stirling's father sent him a letter from Chicago just a few days ago." She paused for impact. "And it had twenty dollars in it! His mother gave ten dollars to my mother."

Everyone gasped. *Twenty dollars!* they whispered in amazement.

"Well," sneered Roger. "That's good news for *your* family then, Kit, since your father doesn't have a job *or* any money. My father says your dad used up all of his savings to pay the people who worked at his car dealership, which was stupid. No wonder no one will offer him a job."

"That's not true!" said Kit, outraged. "My father has job interviews all the time. Almost every day he has big, fancy lunches and meetings about jobs. He'll get one any day now. He said so."

"No, he won't," said Roger. "Nobody wants your father."

With that, Roger shoved his armful of sticky turkey feathers at Kit, who shoved them right back. Kit was so angry and shoved so hard that Roger staggered backward, lost his balance, and fell against a ladder that had a bucket of white paint on it. Everyone shrieked in horror and delight as the can fell over, splattering white paint on the backdrop and clonking Roger on the head! White paint spilled over Roger's hair and face and shoulders and back and arms. It ran in rivers down Roger, striping his legs and his socks and pooling into white puddles around his shoes.

"Arrgghh!" Roger roared. He swiped his hand across his face to clear the paint out of his eyes and lunged for Kit.

But at that very instant, Mr. Fisher appeared. "Stop!" he shouted.

Roger stopped. Everyone was quiet.

Mr. Fisher frowned as he surveyed the white mess. "Who's responsible for this?" he demanded.

"Not me!" said Roger. "Stirling started it. He stuck feathers on me. And then Ruthie called me Mr. Tur—a stupid name—and Kit shoved me into the ladder. *They* did it, not me. They—"

Mr. Fisher held up his hand. "Quiet," he said. "Roger, go to the boys' room and clean yourself up. Boys and girls, I want you to go back to the classroom and sit silently at your desks. Kit, Ruthie,

Everyone shrieked in horror and delight as the can fell over, splattering white paint on the backdrop and clonking Roger on the head!

and Stirling, you three stay here. I want to talk to you."

Roger scuttled past Kit on his way out. "*Now* you're going to get it," he hissed at her, sounding pleased. "*Now* you'll be sorry!"

Kit lifted her chin. "I'm not sorry I shoved you, Roger," she said. "I'd do it again, no matter what the punishment is. I'd shove anyone who says anything mean about my dad!"

"So watch out!" added Ruthie for good measure.

Roger made a face. But for once, he made no smart remark in reply.

When Kit, Ruthie, and Stirling were walking home from school later, the girls agreed that Mr. Fisher's punishment was not too terrible, really. They'd had to clean up the stage, and they were going to have to spend their recess time for the rest of the week helping Stirling redo the backdrop where white paint had spattered on it. Mr. Fisher had also decided that Kit, Ruthie, and Stirling would deliver the class's Thanksgiving basket to a soup kitchen while the rest of the class was watching the Thanksgiving pageant.

"The only bad part of the punishment is missing

the pageant," said Ruthie. "Especially because we have to go to a soup kitchen instead."

"The worst part to me is that loudmouth Roger isn't being punished," said Kit. "It's not fair. He's the one who started the whole fight."

"Don't worry," said Ruthie. "In fairy tales, bad guys like Roger always get their comeuppance in the end. Everyone finds out the truth eventually."

That reminded Kit of something. "Uh, Stirling," she said. "It would probably be better if we didn't say anything about this . . . this situation when we get home. My mother might get a little upset if she found out."

"Mine, too," said Stirling. His voice was serious but Kit saw a little ghost of a smile flicker across his face. She understood. They both knew that Stirling's mother would go into absolute *fits* if she found out her little lamb had been part of a fight. And she'd surely come swooping down to school and insist that he couldn't possibly go to a soup kitchen. Think of the germs!

"You know, Stirling," said Ruthie. "I think you're being pretty nice about this whole thing. After all, it was your drawing that was ruined by all that paint."

Another smile flickered across Stirling's face. "Too bad the first Thanksgiving didn't take place during a blizzard," he said in his low voice. "Then Roger could have been the Abominable Snowman in the pageant."

Ruthie laughed. And Kit did, too.

Stirling knew how to keep quiet. He did not spill the beans about the spilled paint, the fight, or the punishment. So when the day came for the trip to the soup kitchen, Kit and Stirling went off to school as if it were a normal morning. They did bring Kit's wagon with them, but the grownups were too busy to notice.

After an early lunch at school, the rest of the class went to the pageant. Mr. Fisher helped Kit, Ruthie, and Stirling put the Thanksgiving basket into the wagon. It was heavy. Students had brought potatoes, beans, and apples. There were a few jars of preserves and six loaves of bread. Kit and Stirling brought a can of fruit, and Ruthie, whose family still had plenty of money, brought in a turkey that weighed twenty pounds.

"The soup kitchen is down on River Street," said Mr. Fisher. "After you deliver the basket, you may go home." He paused. "Happy Thanksgiving," he said. Then he hurried off so he wouldn't miss the beginning of the pageant.

Kit, Ruthie, and Stirling set out. It was a cold day. The sky was the grayish brown color of a dirty potato, and soon it began to spit rain. Ruthie propped her umbrella up in the wagon to keep the basket dry. Kit's shoes were wet through, and her wrists were wet and chapped because her arms were too long for her coat sleeves. Her shoulders ached from pulling the heavy wagon. But Kit was not the kind of girl who wasted time feeling sorry for herself. Instead, she made up her mind to pretend that she was a newspaper reporter. As she walked along, she imagined how she would write about the people and things she was seeing.

"I'll take a turn pulling the wagon now," Ruthie offered after a while.

"Thanks," said Kit. She smiled at Ruthie, who looked like a damp, overstuffed couch in her new winter coat. "This whole thing is kind of an adventure, isn't it?"

"Sure," said Ruthie, after only the tiniest

hesitation. "We're like the bedraggled princess in 'The Princess and the Pea.'"

Kit grinned. *Good old Ruthie,* she thought. *She has a princess for every occasion.*

"No one who sees us would know that this is a punishment," Kit said. "It doesn't look like one, or feel like one, either."

"No," said Ruthie. "Especially since Roger's not with us."

The girls giggled.

But they stopped giggling when they turned the corner onto River Street and saw the line outside the soup kitchen. It was four people across, and it stretched from the door of the soup kitchen all the way to the end of the block. The people stood shoulder to shoulder, hunched against the rain. The brims of their hats were pulled low over their faces as if they were ashamed to be there and did not want to be recognized. The buildings that lined the street were as gray as the rain. They seemed to slump together as if they were ashamed, too.

"Oh my," said Ruthie quietly.

Stirling didn't say anything, but he moved up to be next to the girls.

Kit prided herself on being brave, but even she was daunted by the dreary scene before her. She squared her shoulders. "Let's go around to the back door," she suggested. "That's probably the right place to make a delivery."

Kit led the way down a small alley and around to the rear of the building. She knocked on the back door. No one answered. Kit lifted the basket out of the wagon. She took a deep breath, pushed the door open, and stepped inside. Stirling and Ruthie followed her. When they went in, they saw why no one had answered Kit's knock. It was very busy.

People were rushing about with huge, steamy kettles of soup, trays of sandwiches, and pots of hot coffee. A swinging door separated the kitchen from the room where the food was served and the groceries were given away.

One lady saw Kit and the others and stopped short. She peered through the steam rising off the soup she carried and asked, "May I help you?"

"We're from Mr. Fisher's class," said Kit. "We have a Thanksgiving basket to donate."

"Oh, yes!" said the lady. "You're expected. Bless you! As you can see, my hands are full. You'll have to unpack the basket yourselves. Leave the turkey and the potatoes and all here in the kitchen. We'll use them to make tomorrow's soup. But bring the canned goods and the loaves of bread out front now. You can give them away."

Kit, Ruthie, and Stirling did as they were told. After they unloaded the basket, they pushed through the swinging door from the kitchen to the front room, which was crowded with people. It smelled of soup and coffee. At round tables in the center of the room, people sat eating and drinking. Some talked quietly. But most of the people kept a polite silence, as if they did not want to call attention to themselves or make themselves known to anyone around them. Along one side of the room, there was a long table with people lined up in front of it. Kit could see only their backs as they stood patiently, holding bowls and spoons, waiting for soup to be served to them. Across the room there was another long table where a lady was handing out groceries and loaves of bread for people to take home. Rather shyly, Kit, Ruthie, and Stirling went over, put their food on the table, and stood next to her.

"Thanks," said the lady. "Please give the bread to the people as they pass by."

Kit, Ruthie, and Stirling kept their eyes on the bread as they handed it out. It was kinder and more respectful not to look into the faces of the people, who seemed grateful but embarrassed to be accepting free food. Most of them kept their eyes down, too. Kit felt very, very sorry for them as they took their bread, murmured their thanks, and moved away. *All of these people have sad stories to tell,* she thought. *They weren't always hungry and hopeless like they are now. How humiliating this must be for them!*

The lady handing out the groceries seemed to know some of the people. "Well, hello!" she said to one man. "You're here a little later than usual today."

Kit handed the man his bread.

"Thank you," he said.

Kit looked up, bewildered.

It was Dad.

KIT'S HARD TIMES

"Kit!" Dad gasped.

Kit couldn't breathe. She felt as if she had been punched hard in the stomach. Shock, disbelief, and a sickening feeling of terrible shame shot through her as she stared at Dad.

Suddenly, Kit could bear no more. She pushed past Ruthie and Stirling and bolted through the swinging doors. She ran through the kitchen and past the stoves with kettles of soup that had billowing clouds of steam rising from them. She burst out the back door into the alley. Once she was outside, her legs felt wobbly, and she sagged against the hard brick wall.

In a moment, Ruthie and Stirling were beside

her. "Kit?" said Ruthie gently. "Are you okay?"

Kit nodded. She looked at Ruthie. "Is my dad still . . ." she began.

"Your dad left," said Ruthie. "He said he'd talk to you at home."

Kit took a shaky breath.

"Come on," said Ruthie. "Let's go." Stirling grabbed the wagon handle, and they started down the alley with the empty wagon rattling and banging noisily behind them. Slowly, miserably, and without talking, the three of them walked together until they came to the end of Ruthie's driveway. They stopped next to the stack of lumber left over from the new garage, and Ruthie turned her sad face toward Kit. "Listen," she said. "Everything's going to be all right."

"All right?" Kit repeated. She shivered. "No, Ruthie," she said. "Everything's *not* going to be all right. My father hasn't been having job interviews. He's been going to a soup kitchen. He had to, just to get something to *eat*, to get food for our *family* to eat." Kit's voice shook. "Dad's not going to get a job here in Cincinnati. Maybe he would have a better chance of finding one in Chicago. I guess . . ." Kit faltered, then went on. "I guess now I hope that he *will* go."

"No, you don't," said Stirling in his husky voice.

Kit frowned. "What do *you* know about what I want?" she asked. "*Your* father is in Chicago, sending you letters with money stuck in them!"

"No," said Stirling. His gray eyes looked straight at Kit. "He isn't."

"What are you talking about?" asked Kit. "I saw the money!"

"That was *my* twenty dollars," Stirling said. "My father gave it to me before he left. He told me to save it for an emergency." Stirling sighed, and then he poured out the whole story. "My mother hasn't been able to pay any rent since we moved in," he said. "I offered her the twenty dollars lots of times, but she always said no. Then, a few weeks ago, she told me that we were going to have to leave your house. I knew it was because she was ashamed to stay any longer without paying. She wouldn't feel so bad if she could help with the housework, but your mother won't let her. I figured if I could trick her into taking the twenty dollars, she might use it for rent. So I made her think it came in a letter from my father."

Kit squinted at Stirling, trying to understand.

"You sneaked the money into the letter?" she asked.

Stirling shook his head. "No," he said. "It's worse than that." He paused. "I wrote the letter myself. I typed it on your typewriter."

"*What?*" Kit and Ruthie asked together.

"The truth . . ." Stirling hesitated. "The truth is, I don't know where my father is," he said. "But I'm pretty sure he's never coming back here to my mother and me. He flew the coop, as Roger said."

"Oh, no," Ruthie sighed.

Kit felt her hands clench into fists.

"So that's how I know that you don't want your dad to go away, Kit," said Stirling earnestly. "No matter what, it's better to have your dad at home. No matter how bad or hopeless things are, you don't want him to leave."

Kit sat down hard in the wagon. She held her head in her hands.

"Stirling," said Ruthie, "you'd better tell your mom what you did."

Stirling nodded. It was as if he'd used up all his words.

Ruthie walked up her driveway backward, waving good-bye until she went inside her house.

48

Kit stood up tiredly. As she trudged slowly home with the wagon and Stirling behind her, a new thought presented itself. *When Stirling tells his mother about the letter and the money, they'll leave,* she thought. She walked up the steps and opened her front door. *They won't live here in our house anymore.*

Of course, Kit had wanted Stirling and his fussbudgety mother to leave ever since they'd arrived. But now . . . It was very peculiar. Now that it was about to happen, Kit did not feel glad. She stood in the front hall, which smelled of wet wool coats and dripped with umbrellas, and watched Stirling head upstairs to the room he and his mother shared.

"Is that you, lamby?" Mrs. Howard called. "Did you wipe your feet?"

Stirling looked back over his shoulder at Kit, and a quicksilvery smile slipped across his face. Then he turned away and climbed the rest of the stairs.

Slowly, Kit took off her coat and headed upstairs to change out of her school clothes. As she passed by Mother and Dad's room, the door opened.

"Kit," said Dad. "Come in here, please. I'd like to talk to you."

Kit went in and sat on the desk chair.

"I've already told your mother about what happened today," said Dad. "I owed her an apology, and I owe you and Charlie one, too. I'm sorry I misled all of you. I should have told you what I was really doing." Dad walked over to the window and looked out. "I've been going to the soup kitchen for weeks now, to eat and to get food to bring home. We've been so short of food. It was the only way I could contribute to the household."

"Are we . . . are we really that poor?" asked Kit, almost in a whisper.

"Yes," said Dad. "We are. But I didn't want any of you to know. That's why I pretended not to be hungry here at home. I'd have lunch at the soup kitchen, and then I could give my breakfast or dinner away to make our groceries stretch further." Dad turned to face Kit. "I shouldn't have led you to believe that I'd find a job here in Cincinnati soon. I guess my only excuse is that I wanted it to be true."

Kit went to stand next to Dad. He put his arm around her shoulder.

"But," said Dad, "it's time for me—for all of us—to face the truth. And the truth is that there's

"It's time for me—for all of us—to face the truth," Dad said.

nothing for me to do here. There's no point in studying the want ads in the newspapers every day for a job that's never going to appear. So your mother and I have decided. I'm going to Chicago."

"Oh, Dad!" cried Kit. "You're not going to Chicago because of that letter from Stirling's father, are you? Because—"

Dad held up his hand to stop her. "I'm going," he said, "because there's really no alternative. We don't have room in the house to take in as many boarders as we need. If I go to Chicago, maybe I can find a job and send a little money home."

"I don't want you to go, Dad," Kit said desperately.

"You'll have to write to me and tell me what happens after I leave," Dad said, smiling a small smile. "It'll be like the old days. Remember the newspapers you used to make for me? I loved them so much. When I'm gone, will you write newspapers and send them to me so I won't feel so far away?"

Kit nodded slowly.

"That's my girl," said Dad. "You were my reporter during the good times. I need you to be my reporter during the hard times, too."

Hard times, thought Kit dully as she left Dad and walked down the hallway. The odor of onions frying rose up from the kitchen, and Kit knew that Mother must be making another one of the odd sauces she made so often nowadays—one that was meant to stretch a small piece of meat to feed a crowd. Kit heard Miss Hart and Miss Finney laughing in their room and Mr. Peck teaching Charlie to play his big double bass fiddle. She thought about the chores waiting for her that absolutely had to be done. Mother needed her to set the table for dinner and scrub the potatoes and put them in the oven to bake. Then there was laundry to iron and fold and put away, all before dinner. *This is it,* Kit thought. *This is the truth of my life now. Maybe forever.*

With heavy, defeated steps, Kit climbed the stairs to the attic. How foolish she had been to think that her life was going to go back to the way it used to be! Kit sank into her desk chair. She cleared a space between her typewriter and a pile of papers and rested her head on her arms. She had been wrong about so many things! Instead of resenting the boarders, she should have been grateful for them.

Instead of wanting them to leave, she should have been trying to figure out a way to fit more boarders in the house. Because . . . Kit felt pinpricks of fear up her spine. Because there was no guarantee that Dad would be able to find a job in Chicago, either. What would become of her family? How would they have enough money for food and clothes and heat? Would they be so poor they'd be kicked out of their house?

Oh, I wish we had room for more boarders! Kit thought passionately. *Then Dad could stay. If Ruthie's right about wishes, and you have to work hard to deserve them, then I promise to work as hard as I possibly can to make this one come true.*

Kit felt a drop of water on her hand. She looked up and saw a new leak in the roof, right above her desk. Drops of water plopped onto the papers next to her. Kit saw that the drops had blurred one of her tree house sketches. *Oh well, what difference does it make?* she thought, shoving the papers aside. *Dad won't be here to build it. There's no use for the sketch or Ruthie's lumber now.* Kit sat bolt upright. *Unless . . . wait a minute! Tree house? Boarding house?*

Suddenly, Kit had an idea.

All through dinner Kit was distracted, thinking about her idea. The more she thought about it, the better she liked it. As soon as they were alone in the kitchen, washing the dishes after dinner, Kit presented her idea to Mother.

"Mother," she said, "I've been thinking. Ruthie's father has a stack of lumber left over from their new garage. He said Ruthie and I could have it to build a tree house. But I bet he wouldn't mind if we used the lumber to fix up Charlie's sleeping porch instead. If we made it nice enough, then maybe Mr. Peck would move in with Charlie."

"And then?" Mother asked.

"Then we could put two new boarders in Mr. Peck's room," said Kit.

"We could certainly use the money," said Mother. She sighed tiredly. "But I just don't know if I could handle the extra work that two more boarders would be." Her face looked sad. "Especially after your father leaves."

"How about asking Mrs. Howard to help you with the housework instead of paying rent?" asked

Kit. "I'd still help, too, of course. But Mrs. Howard is a crackerjack cleaner."

Mother shook her head. "I'm not sure she'd agree to that," she said.

"Oh, I think she would," said Kit. "Stirling says she *wants* to help."

Mother was quiet for a thoughtful moment. Then she said, "Kit, dear, it's very ingenious of you to have thought of all this, and it would be very nice of you and Ruthie to sacrifice your tree house lumber. But I'm afraid lumber for the renovation is not our only problem. We don't have money to pay a carpenter. Who'd do the work?"

Kit sighed and sat down at the kitchen table, discouraged. Then, suddenly, she and Mother looked at each other. They'd both had the same idea at the same time. Together they said, "Dad!"

"Dad could do it!" said Kit. "He's great at building things."

"Yes," agreed Mother. "But the idea would have to be presented to him in just the right way. Now that he's decided to go, it'll be hard to change his mind."

Kit grinned from ear to ear. "You leave that to me," she said, full of enthusiasm. "I have a great plan!"

Mother smiled at last. "All right," she said. "Give it a try!"

"Thanks, Mother!" said Kit. She hugged Mother, and then darted out the kitchen door and flew up the stairs two at a time. She couldn't carry out her plan alone, but she knew just whom to ask for help.

Kit knocked on Stirling's door.

"Yes?" said Mrs. Howard. When she opened the door, Kit saw that the room was as neat as a pin.

"May I please speak to Stirling?" asked Kit.

Mrs. Howard began to say no. "He's very tired, and—"

But then Stirling appeared from behind his mother.

"Stirling," said Kit, looking straight at him. "Will you help me?"

"Yes!" said Stirling immediately. It was as though he'd been waiting for Kit's question for a long time.

The next morning, when Dad sat down to breakfast, this is what he saw at his place:

The Hard Times News

SPECIAL THANKSGIVING DAY EDITION

****

Editor: Kit Kittredge
Artist: Stirling Howard
Adviser: Mothxx Margaret Kittredge

WANTED

Tall bearded man to share sleeping
porch with early rising, agreeable
teenager. Must play double bass and an
drink coffee. Call Charlie Kittredge.

WANTED

Do you have interesting, xexciting stories
to tell about adventures in nursing? If so,
I'd like to hear them! Call Kitk Kittredge.

WANTED IMMEDIATELY

Talented handy man to fix sleeping porch
so xkax it will sleep two. Great workingg
conditions! Call the Kittredge family.

WANTED

Neat and tidy lady to help with housekeeping in exchange for room and board.
Call Margaret Kittredge..

WANTED

Kids with wagon to haul away xxx
leftover lumber suitable for use in fixing
sleeping porch. Call Ruthie Smithens.

Kit, Stirling, and Mother sat on the edges of their seats watching Dad read *The Hard Times News*. When he finished reading, Dad glanced at Mother over the top of the paper with a questioning look in his eyes. Mother smiled and nodded, then Dad smiled, too.

"Well!" said Dad, patting the paper. "Look at this! There's a construction job in these want ads. A boarding house needs to expand. It's right here in Cincinnati, close to home." Dad winked at Kit. "In fact, it *is* at home. It's the perfect job for me!"

Kit ran to Dad and hugged him. "So you'll stay, then?" she asked.

"Yes," said Dad. "I'll go talk to Ruthie's father about the leftover lumber today." He handed Kit's newspaper to Mrs. Howard. "I think there's a job here that might interest you, Mrs. Howard," he said.

Mrs. Howard read the want ads and exclaimed, "My land! So there is!" She turned to Mother. "I'd love to help you with the housekeeping," she said. "I'm very good at dusting. I've noticed that the upstairs hallway—"

"That's Kit's job," Mother interrupted politely. "But with two more boarders moving in soon, there'll be plenty to do. I'd be glad to have your help."

"I'll start today!" said Mrs. Howard.

Kit stood next to Dad and looked around the breakfast table as the newspaper was passed from hand to hand. Charlie and Mr. Peck were laughing and talking together about being roommates. Miss Hart and Miss Finney were beaming at her, looking as if they were brimming over with stories to tell. Suddenly, she heard a quiet voice next to her say, "Happy Thanksgiving, Kit."

It was Stirling. His gray eyes were shining. Kit smiled. "Happy Thanksgiving, Stirling," she said.

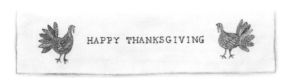

HAPPY THANKSGIVING

Looking
Back
1934

A Peek Into
the Past

When Kit was in school in the early 1930s, students were separated by grade into individual classrooms, just as they are today. They sat in sturdy desks that were nailed to the floor in neat rows, and they stood every morning to recite the Pledge of Allegiance. Boys and girls formed orderly lines to go in and out for recess. Classrooms were quieter and teachers were stricter than they are today.

Children in Kit's time studied many of the same subjects students do today— reading, spelling, arithmetic, geography, and history. Special subjects, such as art, music, and physical education, were taught by teachers who

Report cards in the 1930s often included grades for behavior and attitude.

visited individual
classrooms once or
twice a week. One of
the special weekly subjects in the
Cincinnati school that Kit attended
was *penmanship*, or handwriting.

However, the Great Depression
that had started in 1929 was beginning
to affect every part of society, including
schools. As the Depression deepened
and more people lost their jobs and
homes, schools started having serious
money troubles, too. By 1932—three years into the
Depression and the year Kit's story begins—many
schools could no longer afford new books and
supplies. In some schools, broken windows were
not replaced and roofs started to leak. To save
money, school boards canceled special programs,
such as kindergartens, and shortened the school
year by making school holidays longer
and closing schools earlier in the year.

Some states had so little money that
the school year lasted only three months!
In especially depressed areas—such as the
rural South, where a lack of rain caused
many farms to fail—schools simply closed
down when their money ran out.

*Cincinnati students learned
penmanship by the Palmer
Method and received special
merit pins as they improved.*

*Elementary textbooks from the
1920s and early 1930s*

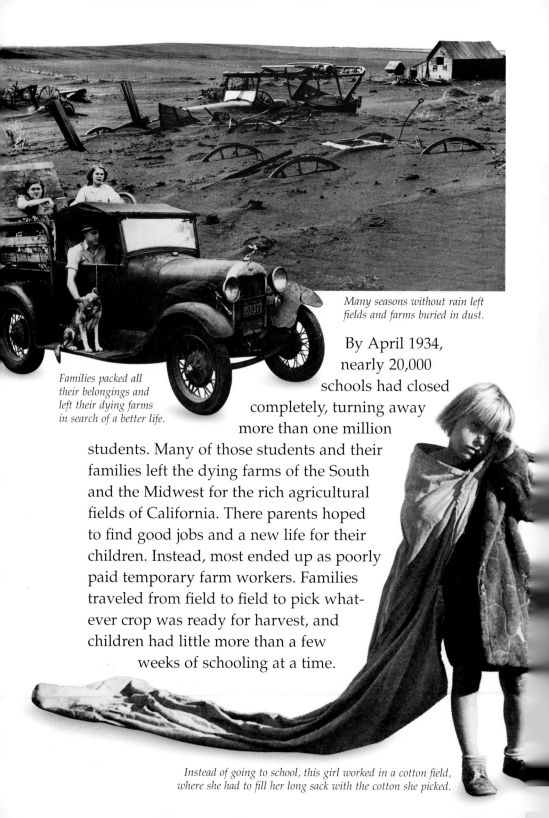

Many seasons without rain left fields and farms buried in dust.

Families packed all their belongings and left their dying farms in search of a better life.

By April 1934, nearly 20,000 schools had closed completely, turning away more than one million students. Many of those students and their families left the dying farms of the South and the Midwest for the rich agricultural fields of California. There parents hoped to find good jobs and a new life for their children. Instead, most ended up as poorly paid temporary farm workers. Families traveled from field to field to pick whatever crop was ready for harvest, and children had little more than a few weeks of schooling at a time.

Instead of going to school, this girl worked in a cotton field, where she had to fill her long sack with the cotton she picked.

Teachers in Chicago protested salary and school cuts.

Before the Depression hit, the average teacher's salary was about $155 per month, or almost $8 per day. To save money without closing schools, some states cut teachers' salaries. In Iowa, teachers were paid only $40 per month, or about $2 per day.

But even after salary cuts, some schools didn't have enough money to pay their teachers. Many teachers went without pay for months. Schools in some southern states revived the old practice of *boarding round* their teachers—giving them rooms and meals with the families of their students in place of a salary.

To further reduce expenses, principals were dismissed and more students were crowded into each classroom so fewer teachers were needed. Many married women teachers were fired so single women or men with families could have their jobs. When programs were cut, other teachers lost their jobs.

Tragedy struck the Cincinnati schools in 1932, when a penmanship teacher killed himself after learning that the school board had eliminated his citywide handwriting program and most of his salary.

Teachers worried when students stopped coming to school, because it often meant that a family was in deep financial trouble or had moved away to look for work. Teachers knew that children sometimes stayed out of school because their shoes and clothes were too worn or they had no money for supplies. They also knew that during the cold winter months, children sometimes took turns going to school because their family had only one presentable coat.

Crowded classrooms made learning hard for students and discipline a challenge for teachers.

Like Kit's teacher, many teachers coordinated food and clothing drives in their communities. Teachers worked with the Red Cross, the Salvation Army, or local

At a food drive, people sometimes received fresh produce, eggs, and cheese in addition to bread or canned foods.

A bread line in New York City

charities to help those in need. They also contributed to funds that collected money for their students and their students' families. Dedicated teachers did whatever they could to help students get a good education as they coped with the harsh realities of lost jobs, daily hunger, and America's uncertain future.

Teachers went to great lengths to help students forget their troubles for a few hours. This class's teacher made sure everyone in the band had costumes.

THE BOOKS ABOUT KIT

MEET KIT • An American Girl
Kit Kittredge and her family get news that
turns their household upside down.

KIT LEARNS A LESSON • A School Story
It's Thanksgiving, and Kit learns a surprising
lesson about being thankful.

KIT'S SURPRISE • A Christmas Story
The Kittredges may lose their house.
Can Kit still find a way to make Christmas
merry and bright for her family?

Coming in September 2001

HAPPY BIRTHDAY, KIT! • A Springtime Story

KIT SAVES THE DAY • A Summer Story

CHANGES FOR KIT • A Winter Story

MORE TO DISCOVER!

While books are the heart of The American Girls Collection®,
they are only the beginning. The stories in the Collection come
to life when you act them out with the beautiful American Girls
dolls and their exquisite clothes and accessories.
To request a catalogue full of things girls love, you
can send in this postcard, call **1-800-845-0005,**
or visit our Web site at **americangirl.com**.

Please send me an American Girl catalogue.

My name is_____

My address is_____

City_____ State _____ Zip_____

1961i

My birth date is_____ /_____ /_____ E-mail address _____
                  Month Day Year

Parent's signature_____

And send a catalogue to my friend:

My friend's name is_____

Address_____

City_____ State _____ Zip_____

1225i

If the postcard has already been removed from this book
and you would like to receive an American Girl catalogue,
please send your name and address to:

American Girl
P.O. Box 620497
Middleton, WI 53562-9940

You may also call our toll-free number, **1-800-845-0005,**
or visit our Web site at **americangirl.com**.

BUSINESS REPLY MAIL
FIRST-CLASS MAIL   PERMIT NO. 1137   MIDDLETON WI

POSTAGE WILL BE PAID BY ADDRESSEE

PO BOX 620497
MIDDLETON WI 53562-9940